LETTUCE!

www.brightbearbooks.com

ISBN: 978-0-9915233-2-0

LETTUCE!

Written
and Illustrated by

Diana Kizlauskas

BRIGHT BEAR BOOKS

To Gabe, Raphie

and all their little buddies...

Rabbit planted lettuce.

A patch of lettuce

grew

so **tall** and *wavy*

BIG and THICK,

he wondered what to do.

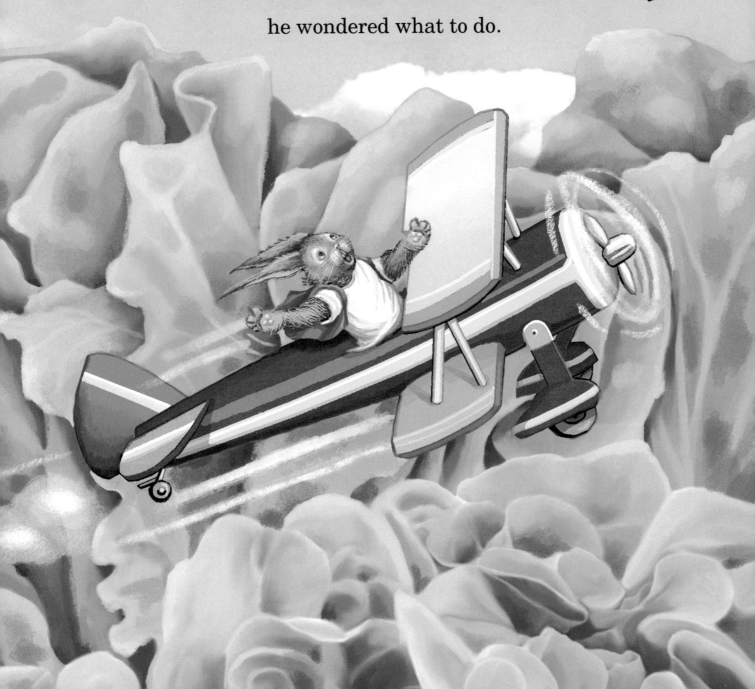

Friends came by to see it.
They said, "Oh, this is

N I C E ! "

Then, one by one,
they tried to help
their buddy with advice.

Cat said, "*Show* the lettuce
for everyone to see.
Win first prize at every fair
and then be on TV!"

Dog said, "*Sell* the lettuce.
Don't set the price too low.
Then take the money to the bank
and watch your dollars grow."

Skunk said, "I smell
B O R I N G!
Let's use it for some *fun*!"

"It's like a
leafy mountain range
to climb
and ride
and run."

"Hey Raccoon," yelled Beaver,
"it's clear as mud to me.
In summer, we'll play hide-and-seek.
In winter, we can ski!"

"I see," crowed out Rooster,
"a thing to *celebrate*!
This lettuce is a monument
to light and decorate."

Pig just burped and grunted,
"I think you have it made.
If I were you, I'd eat and eat,
then sleep in lettuce shade."

Rabbit's friends got tired.
The sun began to sink.
They all went home to get some sleep.

He went inside to think.

Thinking,

thinking,

thinking...

He phoned Wise Owl and sighed,

"How *does* a fella deal with LUCK?
Can *you* help me decide?"

"No I can't," Owl ranted,
"I'm ill, you silly hare!
I'm cold, I'm old, I'm all alone.
My shelves are almost bare!

House needs paint and fixing,
but WHO-ooo would even care?"

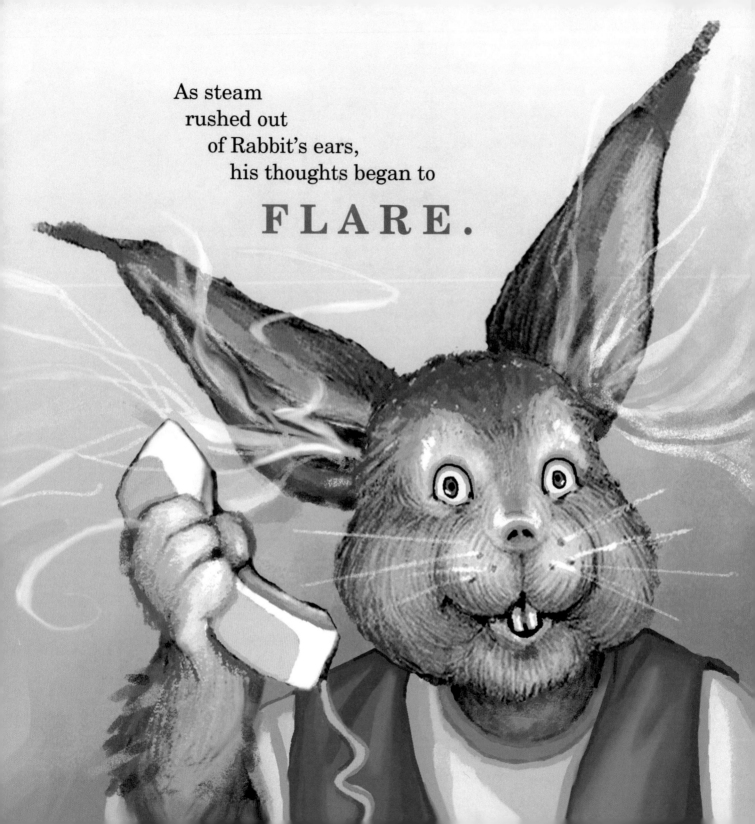

As steam
rushed out
of Rabbit's ears,
his thoughts began to

FLARE.

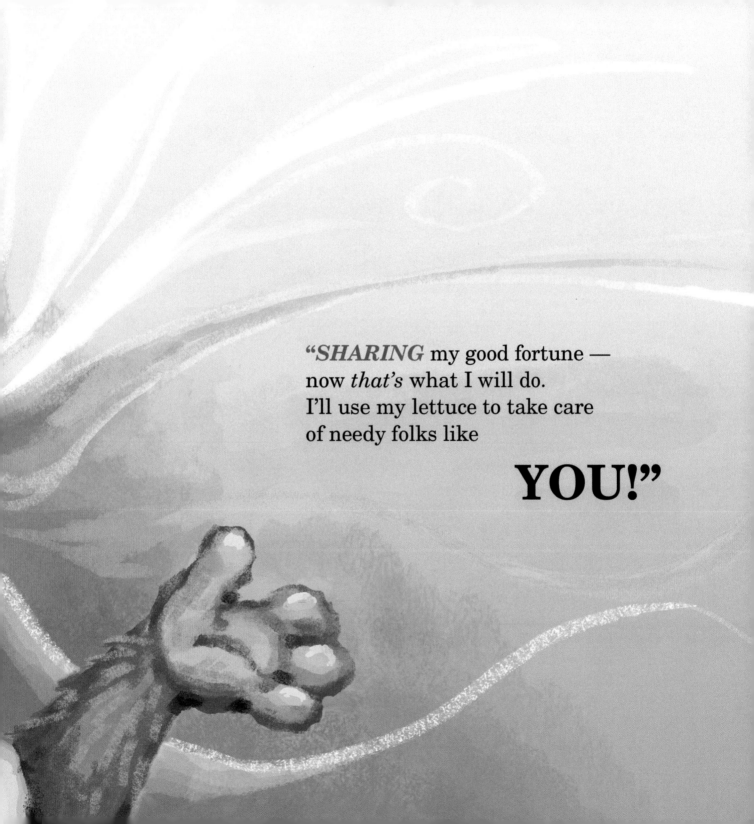

"*SHARING* my good fortune —
now *that's* what I will do.
I'll use my lettuce to take care
of needy folks like

YOU!"

"Thanks, Owl!" shouted Rabbit.
And then he went to bed.
He dreamt how all his lettuce leaves
would keep poor neighbors fed.

Rabbit's pals all helped him.
They cut the lettuce down.
They spread its curly goodness *(yum!)*
across a hungry town.

What was left they traded
to build a Home for Owl,
where nurses took good care of him
and other ailing fowl.

Rabbit's heart was happy.
It lit up with a glow
as big as any lettuce patch
that he would ever grow.

DIANA KIZLAUSKAS

is a Chicago area artist whose children's illustrations have been published by nationally and internationally known companies including Harcourt Achieve; Macmillan McGraw-Hill; Pearson Education/Scott Foresman; Compass/Seed Media; Pauline Books and Media; EDCO/Ireland and others. Most recently, she has both written and illustrated LETTUCE! and Christmas Best, published independently under the imprint of Bright Bear Books.

She is a member of The Society of Children's Book Writers and Illustrators.

Visit Diana at her website:

www. dianakizlauskas.com

Made in the USA
Middletown, DE
24 April 2022

64721748R00022